# WHERE'S THE UNICORN?

# WHERE'S THE UNICORN?

ILLUSTRATED BY PAUL MORAN
ADDITIONAL ARTWORK BY SIMON ECOB, STUART TAYLOR,
AND WAN

WRITTEN BY JONNY MARX AND SOPHIE SCHREY

DESIGNED BY ANGIE ALLISON, JOHN BIGWOOD, ZOE BRADLEY, AND JACK CLUCAS

STERLING CHILDREN'S BOOKS
New York

# INTRODUCTION

The unicorns have had enough of Rainbow Valley. They love playing hide-and-seek, but they've exhausted all of their favorite hiding places and have decided to leave their tranquil forest in search of unbridled adventure.

Ruby, the leader of the blessing (did you know that's the name for a group of unicorns?) has carefully planned a whirlwind tour of the best hide-and-seek sites the world has to offer. One thing is for sure—the unicorns are about to embark on the trip of a lifetime!

Can you find all seven rainbow-colored unicorns in every scene? They are brilliant at hiding, so you'll have to search high and low!

Find the answers plus extra things to spot at the back of the book.

# THE UNICORNS OF RAINBOW VALLEY

## LEAF

Leaf is fearless. He likes adventure and can often be found exploring unchartered areas of the forest. He's always trying to entice other unicorns on his expeditions, but none of them dare follow him into the eerie shadows.

## RUBY

Ruby rules the roost in Rainbow Valley. She loves organizing group trips and days out. She has a big heart and is always there to offer a helping hoof to the other animals in the Valley.

## SNOWFLAKE

Snowflake is a wise and sensitive soul. He doesn't talk much, but he always finds the time to listen to his fellow unicorns and to offer advice. Snowflake is great at hiding and is often the last to be found in games of hide-and-seek.

## BLOSSOM

Blossom is the most sensible of the unicorns. During a game of hide-and-seek, she would prefer to be searching systematically rather than hiding behind a bush or crammed inside a log.

## LUNA

Luna is the fastest unicorn in the land. She loves racing against other animals and is excited to see just how fast creatures outside the Valley can sprint. She dreams of winning a trophy at the Fantastical Tournament for Magical Creatures one day.

## STARDUST

Stardust always has a smile on his face. He fancies himself as a bit of a comedian and is always cracking jokes. He's the youngest of the group and is often the first to get found in hide-and-seek because he can't stop giggling.

## AMETHYST

Amethyst is the cleverest creature in Rainbow Valley. She often has her head buried in a book and is always trying to learn new skills. Amethyst will be going to Unicorniversity next year and she cannot wait.

# SIGHTSEEING

The busy city is a far cry from the tranquility and open spaces of Rainbow Valley, and the unicorns love it. Ruby's organized a packed itinerary for their day of sightseeing. There are so many attractions to see, but she's most excited about visiting the famous bronze Pegasus statue. He's so handsome.

Amethyst has downloaded the audio-guide tour, and is fascinated to learn about the history of different buildings while exploring the city on the hoof.

Can you spot all of the unicorns?

CITY CENTER

# MOUNTAIN BIKING

The unicorns usually ride unicycles, so they are amazed by all the bicycles zooming past at high speed. Luna is sprinting after the other bikers. She wants to finish in first place and win the big trophy.

Daredevil Leaf is in his element, seeking out the highest ledges to jump from. The chaos of clattering wheels is too much for Blossom, though. She's sticking close to the spectators.

Can you spot all of the unicorns?

# FESTIVAL

Ruby managed to get the unicorns tickets to a music festival. She's chatting to some roadies about life on tour, while Stardust is rocking out on stage. Snowflake is feeling apprehensive—he needs the bathroom, but the portable toilets are a bit "unmagical."

Amethyst, on the other hoof, has really let loose—she's right in the action, thrashing her mane about and strutting her stuff.

Can you spot all of the unicorns?

# CAMPING

The unicorns are glad to be back in the woods, but they've never seen a forest as busy or noisy as this one before.

There are hundreds of people in the woodland clearing and they are all chatting, dancing, and playing instruments. Ruby is in the thick of it, roasting marshmallows by the roaring campfire and reveling in the new experience. Blossom prefers peace and quiet and is doing her very best to go unnoticed.

Can you spot all of the unicorns?

# WHALE WATCHING

Brrrrrrrrrrrr! It's a bit chilly out here for the unicorns. They can't even wear woolly hats because of their horns. Nevertheless, Blossom is entranced by the dancing penguins and by the enormous whales.

Snowflake has pranced onto the ice to get closer to the action. He's somehow managed to push a few penguins off their perch and he's trying to apologize before they get too angry.

Can you spot all of the unicorns?

# FIREWORK DISPLAY

BANG! FIZZ! CRACKLE! The unicorns are a bit spooked by the loud noises at the firework display, but Snowflake is in awe of all the bright colors. He wants to get his hooves on a sparkler so he can try writing his name in the air.

Leaf, being the brave creature that he is, is also having a wonderful time. He likes the booming sound of the rockets and the bright glow of the explosions.

Can you spot all of the unicorns?

# MUSEUM

A vacation wouldn't be complete without a trip to the museum. Amethyst is in her element, having a terrific time reading all about ancient civilizations and artifacts. She's even found something that claims to be made from unicorn horn, which has given her the heebie-jeebies!

Luna, on the other hoof, has never been so bored in her life and cannot wait to leave.

Can you spot all of the unicorns?

# ICE RINK

The unicorns have never skated before, and it definitely shows. Stardust hasn't been able to stand up yet, and Leaf has lost count of the number of times he's taken a tumble.

Snowflake is the only one who seems to have mastered the technique. He's performing pirouettes and skating backward. Blossom is a bit miffed, though, at having to rent two sets of skates. It's an expensive hobby!

Can you spot all of the unicorns?

# BEACH

Surf's up and the unicorns are loving the relaxing vibes of beach life.

Blossom is scared to go near the water after watching a documentary about sharks, but Leaf is keen to explore. He's frantically searching for a marine creature called a narwhal, which has a tusk that looks like a unicorn's horn. Amethyst has told him that he's in the wrong continent, whatever that means!

Can you spot all of the unicorns?

THEATER

JUNGLE ROBOT 3

JUNGLE ROBOT 3

# FILM PREMIERE

LIGHTS, CAMERA, ACTION!
The unicorns are hot to trot tonight
after landing themselves an invite to the
biggest film release of the year. Stardust
is making the most of his five minutes
of fame, telling jokes to every celebrity
he meets on the red carpet.

Amethyst and Luna are in competition
to see who can get the most autographs,
while Leaf is steering clear of the spotlight.
He's more interested in the tasty food stalls.

Can you spot all of the unicorns?

# ZOO

The unicorns are in awe of all the incredible creatures that live at the zoo.

Amethyst was chatting with the chimps, but she's now marching with the penguins, trying to communicate through dance and strange-sounding squawks. She's not having much luck. Luna is also captivated. She's testing the elephants' memories by asking them all sorts of questions, such as why are their ears so big, why are they scared of mice, and where did they go to school?

Can you spot all of the unicorns?

# CITY CENTER

Snow is starting to fall in this exotic city and there's a magical feel in the air. The unicorns are delighted that their visit has coincided with a military parade, and some of the unicorns are hoping that the cavalry horses will come by soon.

Ruby and Blossom are busy admiring the colorful domed cathedral, which looks beautiful all lit up in the dark. Luna's had enough of standing still—she's cantering around the edge of the main square trying to keep warm.

Can you spot all of the unicorns?

# ISLAND HOPPING

An island stopover is the perfect place for the unicorns to relax and rest their weary hooves. Ruby is desperate to get out on the water in one of the rafts so she can explore the most remote parts of the island.

Amethyst is in awe of the huge statues that are scattered about. The locals tell her the heads were carved over 1,000 years ago, and she's busy trying to figure out how such gigantic objects were transported to this place all those years ago.

Can you spot all of the unicorns?

# TEMPLE VISIT

Finally, some peace and quiet for Snowflake. He's trotted off into the depths of the temple for some gentle meditation and contemplation. He's blown away by the beauty and precision of the zen garden, and is keen to create something similar when the unicorns return to Rainbow Valley.

Outside is a hive of activity and the other unicorns are marvelling at the wonderful sights—from colorful kites to exquisite traditional costumes.

Can you spot all of the unicorns?

# THEATER

Ruby decided that no trip would be complete without a bit of culture, so she whisks them away to the theater.

Some of the unicorns are treading the boards, putting their acting skills to the test, while others are just as happy to sit and watch while eating ice cream.

Stardust is not happy. Fellow theatergoers keep telling him to be quiet, so he's left the stalls and made his way onto the bright lights of the stage.

Can you spot all of the unicorns?

# SWIMMING POOL

The blessing is having a blast by the pool. Blossom has just been told off for cannonballing, and Stardust is rushing down the slide. Leaf cannot wait for his turn—he's been waiting for what feels like an eternity and is growing impatient. He keeps prodding the person in front of him with his horn, hoping to hurry up the process.

Luna is worried that the chlorine is going to turn her hair green, and she really doesn't want to end up looking like Leaf!

Can you spot all of the unicorns?

# SAFARI

The unicorns are on safari and are having a wild time. Luna is frantically searching for a creature capable of keeping up with her in a sprint. Amethyst has told her about an animal called a cheetah that can run over 60 miles per hour, and Luna is extremely excited.

Stardust is in stitches, laughing hysterically at a funny-looking animal called a warthog. The rest of the unicorns are basking in the brilliant sunshine, relaxing before their long journey back to Rainbow Valley.

Can you spot all of the unicorns?

# ANSWERS

## SPOTTER'S CHECKLIST

- A boy climbing where he shouldn't ☐
- A clown ☐
- A man with a baguette ☐
- A thief ☐
- Three human statues ☐
- Some dropped shopping bags ☐
- A man on roller skates ☐
- A man eating a banana ☐
- A T-shirt with a target sign ☐
- A man on a box giving a speech ☐

SIGHTSEEING

MOUNTAIN BIKING

## SPOTTER'S CHECKLIST

- A barefoot spectator ☐
- Two people clinging on for dear life ☐
- A boy on his father's shoulders ☐
- A rider in a frog costume ☐
- A girl wringing out her T-shirt ☐
- A bright pink bike ☐
- A water fight ☐
- A man doing a wheelie ☐
- Someone being pulled out of the water ☐
- A man carrying his bike ☐

## SPOTTER'S CHECKLIST

Four burly bodyguards ☐

Someone being sick ☐

Two crowd surfers ☐

A group of fairies ☐

A man signing autographs ☐

Roadies playing cards ☐

A tray of burgers ☐

A red and white flag ☐

A man in a purple tie-dyed shirt ☐

A girl in ripped jeans ☐

FESTIVAL

## SPOTTER'S CHECKLIST

A sleeping-bag sack race ☐

Two dogs fighting ☐

A man juggling with fire ☐

A boy scaring his friends ☐

Someone fixing a van ☐

A man climbing a tree ☐

Someone playing the banjo ☐

A telescope ☐

A man telling a ghost story ☐

Marshmallows being toasted ☐

CAMPING

WHALE WATCHING

## SPOTTER'S CHECKLIST

A couple being pooped on by gulls ☐

A man in an eyepatch ☐

A penguin driving ☐

A man with a TV camera ☐

Someone being chased by penguins ☐

Someone holding a fish ☐

A snowboarder ☐

Four pairs of binoculars ☐

A cluster of barnacles ☐

Someone having trouble with boxes ☐

## SPOTTER'S CHECKLIST

A smiley-face poster ☐

A child upside down ☐

A woman carrying a puppy ☐

Five firefighters ☐

A couple with a picnic basket ☐

A woman with pink flowers ☐

Kids with sparklers ☐

A man with a double bass ☐

A girl on a scooter ☐

A man with a guitar on his back ☐

FIREWORK DISPLAY

## SPOTTER'S CHECKLIST

Two men pretending to be airplanes ☐

Someone doing a bear impression ☐

A boy in a tribal mask ☐

A professor with a pipe ☐

A stray cat ☐

A burglar ☐

A boy with a fizzy drink ☐

A child frightened by a tortoise ☐

An old couple reading a map ☐

A man on his laptop ☐

MUSEUM

ICE RINK

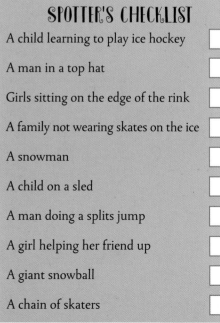

## SPOTTER'S CHECKLIST

A child learning to play ice hockey ☐

A man in a top hat ☐

Girls sitting on the edge of the rink ☐

A family not wearing skates on the ice ☐

A snowman ☐

A child on a sled ☐

A man doing a splits jump ☐

A girl helping her friend up ☐

A giant snowball ☐

A chain of skaters ☐

BEACH

**SPOTTER'S CHECKLIST**

Someone playing Frisbee ☐

A man with a harpoon ☐

Someone with a sore head ☐

A limbo contest ☐

A woman with a tattoo ☐

Kids building a sandcastle ☐

A boy with a fishing net ☐

A man in a red, green, and yellow hat ☐

A purple-and-yellow striped swimsuit ☐

A woman talking on the phone ☐

**SPOTTER'S CHECKLIST**

A woman with green hair ☐

A first-aid kit ☐

A water gun ☐

A man with a walking stick ☐

A TV camera ☐

A girl eating cotton candy ☐

Someone on a motorbike ☐

A man with a purple tie ☐

A woman reading a book ☐

Someone wearing pink glasses ☐

FILM PREMIERE

ZOO

**SPOTTER'S CHECKLIST**

Three escaped monkeys ☐

A stinky wheelbarrow ☐

An elephant being fed a banana ☐

A boy losing his cap ☐

A girl wearing a black beret ☐

A man in a Hawaiian shirt ☐

A boy on his father's shoulders ☐

The odd cat out in the lion enclosure ☐

Six zookeepers ☐

A peacock ☐

## CITY CENTER

## SPOTTER'S CHECKLIST

A woman in sunglasses ☐

A man reading the paper ☐

Three businessmen ☐

A purse thief ☐

A man in a bow tie ☐

A woman with pink hair ☐

A man waving ☐

A group of nuns ☐

A man holding a child ☐

A man in ski goggles ☐

## SPOTTER'S CHECKLIST

A romantic picnic for two ☐

An angry mother ☐

A stingray ☐

A pair of treasure hunters ☐

A game of cards ☐

A boy sucking his thumb ☐

An artist ☐

Men discussing the size of fish ☐

Someone who fell in a hole ☐

A man reading ☐

## ISLAND HOPPING

## TEMPLE VISIT

## SPOTTER'S CHECKLIST

A teddy bear ☐

A sumo wrestler signing autographs ☐

A man with green hair ☐

A stag ☐

A man with a video camera ☐

A couple checking their photos ☐

School children with a samurai ☐

A woman searching in her bag ☐

A girl with a touch-screen phone ☐

A T-shirt with a target symbol on it ☐

## SPOTTER'S CHECKLIST

An actor holding his wig

A mermaid in love

A cold drink being spilled

A man eating messily

An angry old lady

An old man yawning and stretching

Boys playing cards

A girl blowing bubblegum bubbles

A woman covering her ears

A tiny baby

## SPOTTER'S CHECKLIST

Someone fully clothed being pushed in

A woman wearing a sombrero

A man in armbands

A boy with a waterpistol

A man doing butterfly stroke

A pink swimming cap

A human pyramid

An inflatable duck

Two men wearing necklaces

A sunbather having water poured on her

## SPOTTER'S CHECKLIST

A baby elephant

A shy buffalo

A monkey tempted by sandwiches

A leopard-print hat

A lion terrifying tourists

A woman in a stripy top

Three warthogs

A chimpanzee relaxing

A flamingo with a white tail

A thirsty predator

**STERLING CHILDREN'S BOOKS**
New York

An Imprint of Sterling Publishing Co., Inc.
1166 Avenue of the Americas
New York, NY 10036

First published in Great Britain in 2017 by Buster Books,
An imprint of Michael O'Mara Books Limited
9 Lion Yard, Tremadoc Road, London SW4 7NQ, England

First Sterling edition published in 2018.

ISBN 978-1-4549-3166-9

Distributed in Canada by Sterling Publishing
c/o Canadian Manda Group, 664 Annette Street
Toronto, Ontario, M6S 2C8, Canada

For information about custom editions, special sales, and premium and corporate purchases, please
contact Sterling Special Sales at 800-805-5489 or specialsales@sterlingpublishing.com.

Manufactured in China

Lot #:
4  6  8  10  9  7  5
01/19

sterlingpublishing.com